School Days

Table of Contents

Chapters

Note: Attaching your interpretations of each story creates a story's chapter! Begin your interpretation of each Solospaceman story at the end of each Solospaceman story. Then continue it in the Drawing and/or Notepad/Final Copy section found at the end of this book.

-solospaceman-

Watch Solospaceman Animated T.V. Series on website: solospaceman

TM
-solospaceman-
Copyright 2020

-solospaceman-
School Days

My Speech

I was in school working as a teacher. For some reason, I had to leave my school to get something, which I had left home earlier that day. So, after I had obtained from my school Principal's permission to retrieve it, I walked out of my school building and into the surrounding community which lead me straight down a suburban private house block where I made a left turn. There perched in the sunlit horizon I could see my house, so I kept walking towards it. As I was walking there, I slowly began to realize the enormous amount of time it was taking for me to reach my illusive destination. Further, I thought to myself, if I did not turn back now, then I would be late for the next class I had to teach. So, I made another left turn and started walking straight back to my school.

It was a nice day for a walk, and it was about 12:00 noon. Again, as I was walking, the cool breeze really made me feel wonderful especially since I had no hat on my head, and I was dressed in light colored summer garments.
Then all of a sudden and form out of nowhere it started to show. I could not believe that I was seeing snow, until I held out my right hand and felt some snow fall upon it. With that realization also came the realization that I had to move much more quickly than I was previously moving to return to my school on time.

Then, as I looked down the street in which I was walking, I noticed a rather large group of males and females on both sides of it. In the middle of the street, there were all sorts of rows and rows of all kinds of different types of four wheeled cars. But, I was afraid of the people not of the cars, because they looked like they were a mixture of old and young White thugs. Worse, in my mind 's eye, I saw them as a very large horrific horrible obstacle hindrance between me and my school. Consequently, I walked passed them in a hurry then sought refuge in the basement of my school building.

When I got there, it was a cold, dark, and a lonely place. However, it had one bright spot or beacon of light that turned out to be one ray of hope for me. That is, it had an escalator. As I rode it up, my surroundings became brighter and brighter and brighter. Also, people began to appear around it and on it. Some were going down on my opposite side, while others were behind me and in front of me going up on it. Nevertheless, and to my surprise, by the time I had reached the top of the escalator, there were numerous crowds of people of every race, nationality, and religion everywhere. Moreover, it seemed that they were all in a well-lit area of my school building waiting for me to give them either my today's lecture or my today's speech.

(Please place your drawing and/or your interpretation of this story here!)

The Teacher in Charge

I was the teacher in charge, when from out of nowhere at least four of my teacher aids approached me then told me that our school's complex was having a surprise birthday party for one of my honor students inside one of our school's main cafeterias. Then the four of them tried to hide from our complex's surprise party goers and me by not going in the direction of our complex's party and attempting to slip away unnoticed into a section of our school building where many other school extracurricular activities were taking place. When I discovered them on their way there and attempting to not attend our complex's party, I told them that I think that our school's principle would by quite interested in knowing about where they were going during work hours instead of attending our school's complex party.

Surprised by my statement, they turned and faced one another then discussed how best to alter their plans to go to the section of our school building where so many extracurricular activities were taking place. They accomplished that task by changing their directions away from the area in question and walking coolly and calmly with me in the direction of our complex's surprise birthday party until we had reached it. Once there, I saw our students running around in circles, chasing one another, laughing, and playing games or basically just having a whole lot of fun. In fact, on the tables that were set up for the party, there were all sorts of food, party ornaments, and board games on them for their consumption.

However, when I asked the aids in charge of the food distribution if they needed any other food items, they all said that we needed sodas for the kids to drink after they ate and finished their hamburger sandwiches. Then I asked them how many bottles of sodas I should buy. They answered, "Do not buy bottled soda…, but buy twenty cans of soda." After they had explained to me why I should buy cans of soda instead of bottles of soda (the kids did not need glasses to drink out of and possibly break plus can sodas were cheaper to buy then bottles of soda), I agreed to buy them.

So, I asked one of the male aids to go with me to help me find a store to buy can soda from as well as to help me carry the can soda back to the party. He agreed to come with me. Then we started to walk in the direction of the closet store that we thought that we could buy can soda from. Notwithstanding, I was in such a hurry to buy the can soda from the store nearest to us that I walked a few steps ahead of my school aid. When I stopped at a corner and looked both ways to cross its street, I noticed that the aid was missing or not there. So, out of anger, I picked up a heavy rock from the ground that was underneath a garbage container and hit the rock very hard against it. That is when I realized that I could buy can soda from the Associate Grocery Store which was right next to my school building and where my school's complex party was taking place. Consequently, I went to the Associate Grocery Store to purchase the can soda from it and discovered that my school aid was there waiting for me. He was waiting for me inside of the store for two main reasons. One was that he did not know why I had walked passed the Associate Grocery Store. The other reason was that he did not have the authority to buy the can soda for our school's complex party. In fact, I alone had the authority to purchase it, because I alone was the teacher in charge.

(Please place your drawing and/or your interpretation of this story here!)

I walked out of my school Building

I was hungry. I decided to eat some crackers to satisfy my hunger crave. So, I walked out of my school building's side door to catch a local bus to go to my neighborhood's deli and grocery store. Once I arrive there… guess what? A pretty girl I wanted to meet was standing by a pay phone. She looked as if she was waiting to meet someone or to receive a phone call. So, I hide my face under my hat and passed by her pretending that I did not see her, because I had strong feelings for her.

A short time later, I noticed in the same grocery store a group of my young Black male students who should have been in school at the time, but were not. One of them had a brown bag in his hand. It looked like it did not belong to him. So, I asked him to give me the bag and allow me to investigate its origins. At first, he did not listen to me. However, after one of his friends recognized me as Mr. Stephanopoulos his English teacher and instructed him to follow my orders, he gave the bag to me without further incident and with all of its contents intact.

Upon inspecting the item, I discovered that it was filled with consumer legal medical Marijuana from the pharmacy section of the deli and grocery store, but there was no receipt for it. Naturally, I asked the young boy why he did not have a receipt for the Marijuana. He answered me by saying that his dog had chewed it up. So, as I was contemplating my next move, a colleague of mine overheard our conversation and approached us and said that he saw everything that happened with the boy and Marijuana - the boy stole it. He further elaborated that he was going to inform the proper authorities of the incident. So, I traveled at the speed of a ghost rider to return to my school on time, after I had on my own accord walked out of my school building.

(Please place your drawing and/or your interpretation of this story here!)

Just Stop

Many other teachers and I were invited to an auditorium event in our new school building. After the event was over, I lead my class as well as many other teachers and their students back to our classrooms. However, the school building was so new and large and had so many floors and stairs in it that I got lost in it and in turn lost all those who were following me. In fact, at first, when I started leading my class back to our classroom, my students would listen to me and would follow my instructions on how to traverse the new building as we moved from one section of it to the next section of it. Then, after they realized that I did not know where I was going, they stopped following my directions, fell out of line, and distributed themselves without me throughout our entire new school building looking for our classroom. Meanwhile, the teachers and classes behind us stayed well organized, but confused by me misleading them. So, I decided to allow another teacher who was more familiar with our new school building to lead us back to our classrooms, after I told everyone who was following me to just stop.

____

(Please place your drawing and/or your interpretation of this story here!)

Mrs. Pleasant the Classroom Teacher

It all seemed so real; but, after I had awoken up from it, I realized that it was all only just a silly little dream. In the dream, this is what happened. On the very first day of a school year, my former school principal Mrs. Pleasant was a classroom teacher in the school I worked at as an assistance custodian. The school year before that year's first day of school I was a middle school English classroom instructor. Nevertheless, on the first day of that particular school year out of curiosity and to observe a new way of teaching English, I stood in the back of Mrs. Pleasant's classroom as she taught her middle school students' semantics.

At one point during her lesson, I moved myself to the front of her classroom and lend myself on a file cabinet to better observe Mrs. Pleasant's new teaching approach to sentence structure. Then to retrieve an answer to one of her lesson's questions her students had to use the file cards in the file cabinet I was lending on. Consequently, because they saw me leaning on the cabinet and they knew that the year before this current year I was an English teacher, they began to ask me questions about her assignment. So, naturally, because I knew the answers to most of their questions, I started to answer some of them. At that time, Mrs. Pleasant approached me and stated to me that I could not answer their questions, because I was no longer a classroom teacher *but* an assistance custodian. So, I stopped answering their questions and went back to my corner in the back of her classroom to finish cleaning it up.

Then my supervisor, who was wearing a flashy blue business suit while I was dressed in my dark gray custodian uniform, can into the classroom. He had earlier been summoned by Mrs. Pleasant, because a pipe in her classroom needed to be fixed. So, we used the tools in my hand-held toolkit necessary to fix the pipe, but we needed additional tools to completely fix it. Unfortunately, while we were discussing which other tools we needed, another classroom teacher came into Mrs. Pleasant's classroom and started to complain about me to my supervisor. Fortunately, for me, he shrugged her off in an unconventional manner. Then they both left the room while I was left alone to complete fixing the broken pipe with the tools in my toolkit, instead of all the tools I needed to finish the job correctly and completely.

Despite my tool dilemma and once I had finished the job, I did not know what to do next, because it was the first day of my new job as being an assistance custodian as well as it being the first day of the new school year. So, I left the tools we used to fix the pipe in a safe covered tarp area in the center of Mrs. Pleasant's classroom floor. Then I approached Mrs. Pleasant who was simultaneously moving towards me from the rear of her classroom to the middle of her classroom between her students who were evenly and formerly sitting of both sides of us. Oddly, as I approached her and she approached me, she had an opened book in her hands. I could barely see its cover and pages, but she asked me to read it. As I did, something told me that Mrs. Pleasant asked me to read her book to humiliate me in front of her class. For after all, she was the real classroom teacher.

(Please place your drawing and/or your interpretation of this story here!)

Going to College

Going to college can either be frightening, dreadful, or an awe-inspiring experienced event. The question is how one determines which category best fits the decision that he or she made to attend college. Well, one way to establish the correct answer to that question is for the person who decided to attend college to answer more college related questions. For example, he or she might ask themselves… Why am I attending college what is in it for me… then… Am I going to college to learn a trade… a profession… or to socialize and make new friends… What are my learning objectives… What are my learning strengths and weaknesses…? How do my learning strengths and weaknesses affect my specific learning goals…? What should I major in…? Do I have the necessary prerequisite course work to enroll in the major I am considering…? How do I choose the best college to attend that corresponds to my prospective major…? How long will it take me to earn a degree…? More important, do I need financial aid and if I do need it, then where will I get it from, when will I need it, and how much of it will I need?

As a loving uncle, I had to address one of my nephew's concerns about him attending college. So, after asking him to consider his answers to some of the above college related questions, I drove him around our small town in my old and dirty beat-up jalopy, until we had come to Montgomery Berkheimer University which is an "old school" well established educational institution. There, as we got out of my car, people stopped and stared at him, because of his physical disability. That is, he has muscular dystrophy.

Nevertheless, he was impressed with the campus of the college especially after I had explained to him some of its history. So, he went inside of its main building to find out more about it. After he had obtained several flyers, pamphlets, and brochures from the main building's information desk that better explained Berkheimer University's college life, we traveled around the campus sightseeing looking for specific places on campus that were high-lighted in the flyers, pamphlets, and brochures, until we came to its swimming pool where he rolled his wheelchair up the wheelchair access ramp in order to go inside of the swimming pool building and get a better look at its swimming pool. I guess he wanted to see if it was or was not handicap accessible.

At any rate, once I saw that he was safely inside of the swimming pool building, I decided to sit down on one of its many outside public benches, rest for a while, and wait for him to return form the swimming pool area. They say that a flicker in time is worth a dime. So, in order for me to constructively pass this particular moment in our college sightseeing expedition, I started looking into the pool building around the pool area through its many large opened windows and admiring some of its beautiful avant-garde architectural attractions.

When I looked up at one particular section of the pool, I was able to see that it was designated for women's swimming. Then, first, I saw one gorgeous young female model in a bathing suit swaggering her hind parts from left to right as she walked directly in front of me. Then I saw two gorgeous young female models in bathing suits swaggering their hind parts from left to right as they quickly ran pass me to Jack Knife dive into the twenty-one-foot-deep section of the Berkheimer University's swimming pool. Then I saw an uncountable number of gorgeous young female models in bathing suits all studding their stuff around the swimming pool's deck area seemingly without any concern for who or what may be watching them as they frolicked around in it.

Puzzled by their appearances at such a prestigious college as Montgomery Berkheimer, I shook off our unexpected encounter as just another extraordinary example of how quickly our turbulent times cause social change to take place in even our most highly respected conservative institutions. In fact, because I am a product of the Obama Era, I really was shocked to see how liberally those lovely female models openly participated in seductive games at such a conventional collegiate establishment as Berkheimer University especially when I remembered that during the 1960's Berkheimer was one of the few colleges in the United States not to conform to participants of the Hippie Movement request for students to attend its college without uniforms. Also, during the same era, it refused to stop its students from publicly praying in school before they attended their classes. And, of course, Berkheimer University did not allow segregation to permeate its facilities at any time in its long school history. So, again, I was completely baffled to see how openly in public the young female models at Berkheimer University's swimming pool were displaying their accesses as they frolicked around in it.

Regardless of those facts, after firsthand witnessing the cultural and social changes taking place at Berkheimer University, I, myself, decided to apply to attend the college even though that particular decision was completely contradictory to my conservative ways of thinking and made me somewhat of a hypocrite in the eyes of my young nephew. So, because I am a Vietnam Era Vet, I went to the Veterans Administration office at Berkheimer University and explained to one of its many counselors my intentions concerning attending her school. She needed a break from her daily office routine, so we decided to meet inside of the Berkheimer University's main cafeteria. There she told me as we enjoyed our lunch that if I wanted to attend her college, then I would have to mail her the college application that she was handing me by placing a small picture of me on its light green see through envelope. I agreed to do it then reunited with my nephew to explain to him that after answering several college related questions, driving to and around Berkheimer University, sigh-seeing on its campus, and witnessing the social changes that are taking place there, I have decided that we are both going to college.

(Please place your drawing and/or your interpretation of this story here!)

Campus

A black male student and I walked from off campus to on our campus. I was new to the college and as we were walking, he began to explain to me the racial situation at our school. Base on the little knowledge that I had of the school, I thought racism was none existence here, but when we approached one particular school building's entrance we saw a group of white students gathering. One of them threw a black stone at us. It did not hit us, but it did land on the ground near us. In appearance, the small black rock looked like a piece of a meteor. We discussed its significant then I suggested that we should turn around and walk the other way. As we did, we saw two professionally dressed white men wearing all black approaching us. The shorter one instructed us to walk around a corner where they made us show them our ID's. When other black female and male students saw what happen, they too walked around the corner and showed the two white men their ID's and told them of their similar racial experiences on our campus. Later, of course, we figured out that they were plain cloth cops, but we did not know if they were local or governmental agents sent to investigate the racial situation on our Campus.

(Please place your drawing and/or your interpretation of this story here!)

Paranoid State

By bus I took a trip to Moscow. I wanted to find out if weather or not the rumors I had heard about its secret service were true or false. So, when I got there and after I had departed the bus, I stepped inside one of its most top-secret facilities. There I sat inside of a classroom type setting where a Moscow spy instructor drilled not only me, but also several other American enthusiasts who came on the same trip as I did to investigate the secret facility's inner structure.

Then one student disagreed with what the instructor was saying about the facility. So, the instructor accosted him physically by placing him into a wrestler's chock arm to neck hold. When I saw the instructor grab him, I protected his actions by breaking his arm hold on the student. Then the instructor angrily addressed me and my actions by saying that he was less concerned about what I did and more concerned about the KGB agent who was already on his way here to settle our dispute.

When the agent came, he used some type of highly advanced form of communication by telepathically speaking to all three of us at the same time while analyzing the events that just took place inside of the classroom. Then he put images in our heads of each one of us being beaten and stoned by other KGB agents who were displaying their KGB insignia on their uniforms as they beat us. Worse, he physically attacked the student who disagreed with the secret facility's instructor without touching him with his hands or feet.

When the other students in the classroom saw his attack, they all attempted to run outside of the classroom to escape his anger. But, the KGB agent stopped them by moving faster than the speed of sound from in front of the classroom's door entrance to its rear door's way out as a show of force to them. He even ran by me making the motions of hitting me, but he did not hit me… physically. So, I tried to detain him by firing my secret weapon at him which was a pen that was also a 22-ca. gun, but somehow he used his mental technology to impede my afford.

Still, one or two students did make it out of the classroom. There, outside in the topical jungle they had to pass through to get inside of the secret facility, they contacted the USMC by using a hand-held-radio that they had hid there earlier that day in case of an emergency like the one we just experienced. When the US soldiers came, they first appeared to be a large tactical force. However, once they had actually started their assault on the secret complex, we could see that they were only few in numbers or a handful of specially trained Navy Seal marines.

Nevertheless, they entered the facility with their guns drawn. However, just like my attack of the single KGB agent their attack had little or no effect on the gorilla fighting style of the KGB agents who came to combat them with their advance weaponry. So, the small *but* highly trained and equipped USMC squad ran back through the complex's doors then into its outside jungle in a fear-stricken panic in order to escape the incoming KGB attackers' highly sophisticated weaponry. Afterwards, they (the USMC squad) went back to their secret facility base in order to retaliate the next KGB terrorist attack by finding weapons that would overcome the KGB agents and their own *Paranoid States*.

(Please place your drawing and/or your interpretation of this story here!)

I Taught Someone

One day, I was working in my school, when I overheard some teachers talking. They were discussing a poor little boy who needed to be educated. In the past, they and many other teachers had tried to teach the boy, but could not! Because, he lived in such an improvised community that whatever he learned in school on any given day he forgot once he was home. That is, he could not overcome the hostilities or harsh reality of living in extreme poverty despite attending school.

I became interested in educating the boy, once I fully realized his situation. So, after I had made arrangements for us to meet in our library after school, I began to teach him. Our first lesson involved math. I taught him the four basic mathematical operations of adding, subtracting, multiplication, and division. He learned them at a slow paste, but he learned them sufficiently.

However, the more I taught him the more I realized how little I knew about math and the other academic subjects that I was attempting to teach him. As an English teacher, they were outside of my expertise. In truth, the fact was that he needed more and better general subject teachers than me. So, I made arrangements with the teachers who had originally tried to educate him to re-teach him, because I felt that my teaching him after school had finally taught him how to retain knowledge. Therefore, they met with him after school in the same library where I taught him, but on different days of the week and at different times of the week. Of course, with all of the additional teaching he received after school, in time he became a straight "A" student.

In fact, after he had earned a high school diploma, he went on to college and received numerous academic rewards, wed, and became a politician. However, despite his various achievements, he never forgot the basic lessons we taught him. He showed us that by becoming the first Black President of the United States. That is why I tell my children and my grandchildren I am extremely proud of the fact that in my youth I taught someone to be… I taught someone to have…, and without concern for my own academic insecurities… I taught someone.

(Please place your drawing and/or your interpretation of this story here!)

Bad Students

After the close of one particular school day, as a social studies teacher and I were walking from our school to our homes, some disruptive students followed us shouting at us annoying names. Still, when the social studies teacher and I reached our homes, he went into his house and I into mine unashamed. Nevertheless, I am not sure as to why the social studies teacher remained so calm during our frightening ordeal, but maybe it was because he anticipated that he would close his front door behind him very quickly once he had reached it. I do know why I kept my cool. The reason was that I knew inside of my house there was a beautiful woman and her daughter waiting for me to come home.

Still, unlike my neighbor the social studies teacher who lived in our community for many years, I had just moved there. In fact, I had just bought my house form my stepbrother a day or two before our incident with the bad students took place. So, when I got home that day, the women and I walked around the first floor of my new house looking for whatever repairs or renovations it needed, while her daughter Tara cooked dinner for us in the kitchen. As she was cooking, those annoying students came back. So, I went outside to confront them. There they all shouted more annoying names and obscenities at me. After they did, I ordered them to remove themselves from my property. They refused! However, after I informed them that Martha had contacted the police, they left.

Once they had departed, I went back inside of my house to finish enjoying my meal and the two beautiful ladies in it. While I was eating, I remembered that during my ordeal with the bad kids I noticed how damaged and in need of repairs the top parts of my house were. So, after dinner, I went upstairs for the very first time. I wanted to take a second look at the ruins upstairs and on the top of my house. In fact, I brought Martha with me just in case I needed an extra pair of eyes to investigate the inside of my upstairs as well as to reassure me of any repairs it might need.

When we reached the attic, I could not believe how run down, smelly, and water damaged it was. It had dried ice dams and condensation spots left over from last winter's storms. Its roof and its fixtures leaked. Worse, it had mold and wood damage, which caused the structural ruins I saw on the top of my house, when I was outside confronting those awful kids.

However, there was one bright spot upstairs. It had a bathroom with a very large and elegant mirror in it. In fact, when I saw my reflection in the mirror, I better understood why Martha and her daughter were so attracted to me. Still, after considering all of the incongruities I found upstairs, I realized how badly my stepbrother had cheated me. Indeed, I concluded that in terms of morality he had a lot in common with the bad students I met that day.

(Please place your drawing and/or your interpretation of this story here!)

Drawing and/or Notepad

-solospaceman-

Please place your drawing and/or written interpretation of this story here!

Continue…

Final Copy

____

Drawing and/or Notepad

-solospaceman-

Please place your drawing and/or written interpretation of this story here!

Continue…

Final Copy

____

-solospaceman-

Drawing and/or Notepad

-solospaceman-

Please place your drawing and/or written interpretation of this story here!

Continue…

Final Copy

____

www.ingramcontent.com/pod-product-compliance
Lightning Source LLC
Chambersburg PA
CBHW042014110726
48006CB00004B/1089

9798747693357